Out of this World

MONSTER PLANET

by Cally Odgers

illustrated by Georgina Thomas

7000

D0333942

■SCHOLASTIC

THE ARKIES

This 2009 edition published in the United Kingdom by
Scholastic Ltd
Villiers House
Clarendon Avenue
Leamington Spa

Out of this World: Monster Planet
ISBN 978 1407 10114 9

Printed by Tien Wah Press, Singapore

1 2 3 4 5 6 7 8 9   9 0 1 2 3 4 5 6 7 8

Contents

Characters

Singer

Gentle Singer can sense the mind of any living being, and communicate by thought alone. She understands many languages.

Lyam

Science whiz Lyam can tell the Arkies everything they need to know about alien plant and animal life – and then some.

Merlinna

Merlinna is always ready for a battle. She's an expert with weapons – including her naturally piercing screech.

Pace

Pace is a practical guy with a very practical skill – he can communicate with electronic equipment. He and Singer are special friends.

EarthNet

Tench and Farla are EarthNet agents who trail the *Ark3*. They want to capture the Arkies and return them to Earth.

Tench   **Farla**

chapter 1

Under Attack!

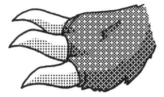

We were in orbit around a new planet. ArkMa was cranky. You might think the electronic brain of a spaceship can't get cranky but ArkMa does. Maybe that's because she's programmed to act like a mother.

"Aw, come on, ArkMa." I said, "I've studied so much this week I'm overflowing."

"The human brain cannot overflow, Pace," said ArkMa. "And you will—"

ArkMa's voice cut off as Merlinna switched her to silent mode.

Later we wished she hadn't done that.

Merlinna winked at me. "OK, Pace. Let's land."

I switched to manual landing gear. Perfecto! As we dropped, everything looked fine. No fog. No pointy mountains. Just nice green, flat, smooth – treetops!

Even through *Ark3*'s reinforced hull we heard the snapping of tree branches as we smashed through the canopy. *Ark3* jarred, juddered and slid sideways. We fell in a heap against the viewscreen, with Singer underneath.

I picked myself up and heaved Lyam to his feet. Then I offered my hand to Singer. She was rubbing her head. "We're still alive, aren't we?" I demanded. "ArkMa, damage report."

ArkMa didn't answer, even when I switched her back to voice mode. Her green lights flashed, so nothing was wrong. ArkMa was sulking.

Lyam checked the air sensor. "Plenty of oxygen."

We finished our landing drill and I tucked the MatterConverter in my belt. Lyam had his sample kit already and Merlinna checked her tangle-line.

"Singer? Any didgies?" Lyam asked. "Or any EarthNet agents?"

Singer is our psychic. Just as I can talk to most electronic minds, she can pick up the live sort.

She closed her eyes and slowly shook her head. No didgies. That was good. It meant the planet wasn't already inhabited by intelligent beings. No EarthNet agents? That was good too. It meant no one would be trying to catch us Arkies and send us home to be "re-educated".

"Let's go!" I did my best to sound positive but I knew I had messed up that landing. I cracked the door open and we stepped out. Fell out, I should say. The flat ground I thought I saw was really a tangle of branches and vines. We fell right through to the real ground over two metres below.

I gave myself a quick check. My ship-suit was torn and I had scratches where branches had whipped past me. My knee hurt but nothing was broken.

I was about to say it could have been worse – when I realised that Singer was still lying where she had fallen. Before I could get to her, we were attacked.

ROARRRRARRRR!

It really did say that. The monster was huge

and horned and hairy, with a green and brown mottled hide, long claws and bony ridges over its eyes.

"Back!" yelled Merlinna. I heard a sharp hiss as she unreeled her tangle-line and zipped it at the monster.

Lyam and I stumbled backwards, hauling Singer with us. Arkie training teaches us to assess situations quickly.

ROARRRRARRRR!

The tangle-line snapped the monster's claws, so it missed us with its first swipe.

It roared even louder. Merlinna drew back the tangle-line and zipped it out again, catching the monster round the nose. The monster jerked back, snatching the tangle-line from Merlinna's hand.

This was getting serious.

"Pace, do something!" snapped Merlinna.

I whipped the MatCon out of my belt.

C'mon, little bro, give us all you've got! I told it. Some people say it's weird to talk to inanimate things but I wanted the MatCon to save our skins. The least I could do was to ask it politely.

Shield! I thought. I raised the MatCon and pointed it at the nearest tree. A few quick bursts and the wood converted into a wide, crescent-shaped screen.

"Bigger!" said Merlinna as I dragged Singer behind the shield. She fell in a heap.

"Can't," I shot back. "If I stretch it bigger, it will get thinner and—"

SWOCKKK! The monster swung its claws straight at the shield. One of them poked right through.

Lyam yelled. "That wood's porous!"

Close up, weave tight, I told the MatCon, aiming at the claw. I felt it fizz with glee. It tightened the wooden shield around the claw so when the monster tried to draw back for another swipe, it couldn't.

AGHHHH! ROARRRRRR! The monster was roaring and thrashing about as it tried to break away. Above the noise I heard the wood beginning to rend.

Maybe you're wondering why I didn't use the MatCon to convert the monster into monster mince? Well, that's against the Arkie rules. The

Ark Masters say MatCons would be terrible weapons if we were allowed to transform didgies with them. Maybe you want to know why I didn't yell to ArkMa for help? Well, she can help us only when we're inside the Ark. *Ark3* doesn't have any weapons.

Now what? I wondered, as the monster didgie raged. I wanted to check if Singer was OK, but none of us would be OK if the clawmonster got loose. Merlinna threw a rock at the creature. Bad move. The rock hit the shield and jarred the claws out of the wood.

WHACK! Clawmonster swiped at the shield again.

Lyam picked up a branch. "Make another weapon – quick!"

With a burst of the MatCon, I turned it into a wooden club. "Find metal!" I gasped.

"This rock?" yelled Merlinna, but I could see there wouldn't be enough metal to make anything useful. Desperately, I told the Mat-Con to make a stone sword. It was heavy but Merlinna whooped and sprang into battle.

chapter 2

N o k o

Singer tried to get up.

Lyam turned on her. "Why didn't you tell us there were monsters about?"

Singer stared. Her face was putty-coloured.

"You said this place was clear!" raged Lyam.

"Stop it!" I snapped. I made another branch into a sharp wooden spear. "Can't you see she's hurt? Singer…" I tried to help her up but Lyam pulled me away.

"If we don't help Merlinna, we're all gonna die!"

Arkie training makes you quick and good at dodging but we were getting the worst of the fight. Clawmonster swung around with a howl

of pain. Its long, spiked tail brushed against Merlinna, knocking her over. Lyam tried to help her up but the monster swerved again.

ZPPPT!

The monster howled. Out of the corner of my eye, I saw someone jump aside. Then whoever it was grabbed the back of my belt.

"It's para-darted. Get moving before it falls on top of you," said a strange voice.

As I turned, the monster reared up on its hind legs, swayed and tipped over backwards. It landed against the shield I'd made.

"Come on!" said the voice. "Get clear."

Lyam and I helped Singer up and did as he said, while Merlinna retrieved her tangle-line.

"Who are you?" asked Lyam.

"Call me Noko," said the stranger. He looked a few years older than us. His hair was tied back from his face and he was wearing skimpy clothes made out of skins. I noticed a big curved knife in his belt. He grinned at us. "Come and meet the others."

I hesitated. Arkies are not supposed to get involved with didgies. It was obvious this planet wasn't S-R, or Settlement-Ready. It might have good soil, water, air and vegetation but it also had didgies. And savage beasts.

Merlinna nudged me. "You heard what Noko said. Let's go."

"What about the rules?" I said. "We should leave straight away."

"Sure," said Lyam. He pointed at *Ark3*, above us in the trees. "But we have to find a way to get back up there, and meanwhile that monster might wake up."

"Let's go," urged Merlinna.

I stuck the MatCon in my belt and fell in behind Lyam and Merlinna. I could hear them chattering to Noko.

I took Singer's arm and we followed the others along a narrow trail. Noko slashed at the vines as he went. They bled sap, so the rest of us ended up covered in purple goo.

"What happened?" I asked Singer. "Why didn't you sense the monster? Or Noko?"

"I bumped my head on the viewscreen," said Singer. "It almost knocked me out."

She did look pale. No wonder she had just shaken her head when Lyam asked about didgies. She had been trying to stay conscious.

"Merlinna likes Noko," she said suddenly as we pushed through some thick scrub.

"Huh?" I said.

"Merlinna thinks Noko is cool. Lyam too."

"What about Noko?" I asked. "What does he think of us?"

Singer frowned. "I can't tell."

That was weird. Usually, Singer can read didgies well. "It must be your headache," I said.

"He's shielding from me." She put her free hand on my arm. "And another thing, Pace – he's not a didgie. He's human, like us. What if he's from EarthNet?"

"He doesn't look like Farla and Tench," I said. "He doesn't talk like them, either."

"Not all EarthNet agents look the same. This could be a trap."

EarthNet agents Farla and Tench hassled us a lot, although we hadn't seen them in the last few weeks. I hoped they'd given up on us – or gone to hassle someone else.

The Monster Planet was hot and humid. Some of the vines had sharp barbed hooks. I was about to ask Noko if he would wait while I repaired our ship-suits, when we stopped at a fence of sharply pointed poles, all smothered in vines.

There was a gap in one part and Noko crawled through.

"I don't like this," said Singer.

I didn't like it either, but Lyam and Merlinna had followed Noko. I heard Merlinna's voice, cheerful and interested, asking questions on the other side.

"We'd better stick together," I said. I helped Singer through the gap.

"Welcome to Stockade," said Noko, grinning. "I'll call the others."

The stockade was completely surrounded by stakes. There were wooden seats around a fire pit, and several hump-shaped buildings. There was also an extra-big building covered with vines. It was so overgrown I couldn't make out its shape.

Noko tossed his knife in the air, caught it again and threw it hard at one of the humped huts.

THOCK!

"Come out, Stockaders. We have visitors!" called Noko.

Three boys, dressed like Noko, popped out of the hut. One of them pulled the knife out of the hut wall and tossed it back to Noko.

As we sat down, I took hold of Singer's hand and nodded to her. Then I gritted my teeth. Singer knows I hate it when she talks inside my mind but I needed her opinion.

Too hard to read, she said. *They're all shielded.*

I let go of her hand. Then I waggled my jaw. When Singer mindtalks, it makes my teeth feel funny.

Noko stoked the fire and one of the others brought a clay pot to set in the coals.

"You're Arkies, right?" said Noko.

chapter 3

The Stockaders

I suppose I looked surprised. "How did you know?"

Noko grinned. "Guess."

"You've met others?" suggested Lyam. He sounded disappointed.

Noko looked at my shoulder patch. "Pace, *Ark3*. You're the electronics expert, right?"

"Sure he is," said Merlinna. "I'm Merlinna – weapons expert."

Noko gave her an admiring look. "You were leading the fight back there with that stone sword."

"My usual weapon is a tangle-line," said Merlinna eagerly.

Noko glanced at Lyam. "You?"

"Lyam. Science geek," said Lyam.

"Well, well." Noko laughed. "And do you sci-guys still bother about testing for toxins and alkaloids?"

"We'd be dead if we didn't," said Lyam.

"We've got a better way to check for poisons," said a tall boy with red hair.

Noko grinned. He grinned and laughed a lot. I was getting tired of it. I like cheerful people but no one should be that cheerful all the time.

I knew he was going to grill Singer next, so I got in first. "Singer is our didgie expert," I said, "but she's got a headache."

Noko pointed to the red-haired boy. "That's Webe, and the other two are Saba and Rudu. We named ourselves when we settled here. New home, new names." His grin got even wider.

"We're from—" began Merlinna.

"Earth," said the red-headed Webe.

"We're all from Earth too..." said the shortest one, Rudu, and yawned. "Boring, over-civilised, over-crowded, over-policed planet!"

"I guess that's why you left as well," said the blond guy they called Saba.

I was about to explain that we Arkies leave Earth because we want to help society when I realised something.

"You're Arkies too," I said.

Rudu yawned again. "Wrong! We were Arkies. We're Stockaders now."

"What happened to your Ark?" I asked.

The Stockaders exchanged glances.

"If your ship broke down, you're welcome to come with us when we leave," I said.

"Who says we want to leave?" said Saba.

"There are monsters here," I reminded him.

"So? We can handle them."

"It's good here," said Webe. "We run things to please ourselves." He leaned forward and stirred the clay pot on the coals. "We have food, water, fun … and we make the rules!"

"Something smells good," put in Merlinna, sniffing.

"But you want to keep on exploring?" I asked. "That's what Arkies are trained for."

Noko laughed (of course). "You've got it round the wrong way, Pace. Arkies are trained to explore and to find new S-R worlds. Well, we found one. And we settled it."

"What about EarthNet?" I said. "Haven't their agents been hassling you?"

"EarthNet?" Noko hooted. "Friends of yours?"

"We hate them," said Merlinna. "They try to spoil everything."

"Well, one of them did visit us but she won't bother us again."

"You can't settle a world with four people," I said.

"We can and we have." Noko then waved his hand at Saba, who began to serve the food in wooden bowls. My mouth began to water at the smell.

"Of course," Noko went on, "we'll need more settlers. Some girls would be good." He winked at Merlinna. "Got to have the right people, though. How about it?"

"Us?" I stared at him.

"Sure. Why not?" Noko flipped his knife in the air and caught it. "You're only kids but you all know how to handle yourselves – even your sci-guy."

Lyam opened his mouth and closed it again.

"No need for you to make a decision this instant," said Noko. "Eat up and we'll show you round."

I had lots of questions but the smell of dinner made my stomach growl with hunger. I decided my questions could wait.

After we'd eaten, we looked around.

"Sleep hut," said Noko. "Food storage hut. Tool hut."

"Is everything inside the stockade?" I asked.

"Well – not everything," said Noko. "There is a swimming hole which is only a few minutes' walk from here. We'll take you there later."

Next, Noko challenged Merlinna to a weapons contest. The rest of us sat and watched as they took it in turns to toss the knife.

"What do you think?" muttered Lyam. "Should we join them?"

"We're Arkies," I pointed out. "Our job is to send a report and move on."

"Noko's right, in a way," argued Singer aloud. "Our job is to find S-R planets, and this one is the best we've seen."

"What about the clawmonsters?" I asked. I was surprised at Singer.

She shrugged.

"Earth has worse things, Pace. No one says Earth isn't S-R."

"We should send a report," I repeated.

"We need to know more. How can we judge from just one small area?"

"We could explore," agreed Lyam.

"Will Noko and his friends let us?"

"Why not?" Lyam sounded surprised. "They can't claim a whole planet for just four people."

I wasn't so sure.

"They said we could join them," reminded Lyam.

THACK!

"They'd be the ones in charge."

"So what? They're more fun than the Ark Masters. At least they're human."

Our conversation was interrupted by Noko's whoop of triumph. He had won the contest against Merlinna – but only just.

He clapped Merlinna on the shoulder. "So, kids, do you want to become Stockaders?"

I glanced at the other Arkies. Lyam looked hopeful. Merlinna was nodding. Singer didn't look sure.

"No hurry," said Noko. He grinned at Merlinna. "Time to restock the larder. Want to come hunting?"

chapter 4

Mind Talk

Noko, Rudu, Webe and Merlinna went hunting. The rest of us stayed at the stockade. I was wandering around, looking at the buildings, when I realised Saba was watching me.

"I'm not going to steal anything," I joked.

Saba didn't smile.

Lyam strolled over to us, carrying a long strand of vine. "These plants have got a really high carb content," he said. "You could just about live on them, even without conversion. Did you use them in that food?"

"No," said Saba.

"The Ark Masters will love these," said Lyam, full of enthusiasm.

Saba sighed. "Let's get things clear, kids. If you decide to join us, there won't be any reports. As far as the Ark Masters are concerned, your ship crashed. You died. And you'll have to switch off your shipbrain."

"But—"

"We've got a good place here," said Saba. "Who wants sci-guys and settlers swarming all over it?"

"What happens if we don't join you?" I asked. I had a bad feeling about this.

"Nothing," said Saba. "You just won't mention us to anyone."

"That seems fair to me," said Lyam. "What do you say, Singer?"

"It sounds fair," said Singer.

I wondered if it would be that easy. If we did decide to go, would the Stockaders trust us not to send a report? And should we make that promise?

When the hunting party returned, Noko, Rudu and Webe were laughing excitedly. They were all carrying bulging bags over their shoulders, and I noticed a MatCon stuck in Webe's belt.

"How did it go?" I asked Merlinna.

"OK," she said. "We got some meat." She didn't look very happy.

"Is everything all right?" I asked.

"Of course!" said Merlinna loudly. "Fine."

After the Stockaders had stored their bags in a hut, they decided to go swimming. Merlinna and Singer wanted to stay behind but Noko wasn't having that. "Come on, kids – we've got the best swimming hole!" he said.

"Monsters?" I suggested.

Noko patted his blowpipe. "Nothing to worry about when you're with me."

He led us through more of the goo-vines and some thick scrub. We'd been walking for a while when I suddenly realised Saba wasn't with us.

"Where's Saba?" I asked.

"He's gone to check on the cells," said Rudu.

"Huh?" I said.

"He's over there." Rudu pointed through the bushes. "Saba keeps his experiments in those. They smell bad. That's why they're not inside the stockade."

"Believe me, you want to stay out of those cells," said Noko with a laugh. "Don't worry about Saba. He'll catch up."

The waterhole Noko showed us was deep and clear. It was a long time since we'd been swimming, but I checked carefully for monsters before I jumped in to scrub the sticky purple goo off. When we got out, I used the MatCon to dry our ship-suits and then mend them. On the way back to the stockade, Merlinna and Singer trailed behind.

"I'll see what's wrong," I said, but Noko stopped me.

"Look, Pace," he said, "Merlinna has decided to join us. She's worried about what you'll say."

I stared at him. Would Merlinna really stay if the rest of us wanted to go? I made up my mind to talk to her about it as soon as I could.

When we got back to the stockade, Noko took me aside. "I hope you join us, Pace," he said. "You're the leader, so I'm sure you can persuade Lyam and Singer."

"I'm not the leader," I said, surprised. "Arkies work as a team."

"That's the official standpoint," said Noko. "But you and I both know someone is always in charge. And in your case, Pace, it's you."

I almost laughed at the idea of Lyam, Singer and Merlinna taking orders from me. I was about to point that out to Noko when Singer stepped into my mind.

Pace, I need you.

The back of my neck prickled. Mostly, Singer touches my hand before she talks in my mind. My expression must have changed, because Noko laughed.

"You look as if an insect bit you!"

I rubbed the back of my neck. "I'll go and talk to Singer. She did say settling planets is what the Arkie programme is all about."

Still rubbing my neck, I wandered over to where Singer was sitting by the fire pit. I grinned at her and touched her hand.

What's going on? What are you doing in my mind?

Sorry, Pace. I couldn't help it. Singer looked as if she was about to cry. *There's something alive in those cells near the swimming hole.*

I nodded, and grinned. I knew Noko was watching us. "So, what do you think about this place?" I said aloud. "Good, huh?"

Are you sure? I added in my mind. It felt really weird, holding two conversations at once.

Singer said she was sure, so we wandered around the stockade until we found Merlinna.

"Chain time," said Singer, so I took one of Merlinna's hands in my free one to form a psychic chain.

What's going on? I asked.

They use their MatCon to kill animals for food, said Merlinna. Then she added, aloud, "But what if the Ark Masters come looking for us?"

I was horrified but I made myself laugh. "I bet the Stockaders could soon get rid of them."

"Of course they could," said Merlinna. She stretched. "It'll be dark soon. Maybe we'd better go back to *Ark.*3 and get some gear."

"No need for that," said Noko, strolling up behind us. "You can camp here in the stockade."

chapter 5

In the Cells

I used the MatCon to make vines into fibre-sheets for two tents and we settled down for the night.

"Well?" said Lyam. "You want to join them?"

"We'll see," I said aloud. I thought Noko and the others might be listening. I'd been lying there for a while, thinking about what Singer had said, when I heard an electronic mind. It reminded me of ArkMa, but the sound wasn't quite right.

Hello? Ma'am? I thought back. I knew the mind was female, just as I know the MatCon is male.

Bad! Bad! said the mind.

Before I could decide what to do, Singer popped into my head again.

Pace? Come.

I groaned.

"What's wrong?" asked Lyam.

"Singer's calling," I said very quietly.

Lyam knows Singer doesn't call without good reason, so he followed me out of the tent. Singer and Merlinna were already waiting for us. We formed a chain. I noticed Singer's hands were shaking.

We're going to the cells, said Singer.

What about the monsters? I asked.

We have to go out sometime ...

Quietly we crept towards the exit of the stockade.

As we passed the big building that was so overgrown, I heard the electronic brain again. *Bad, bad.*

I shook my head. It was bad enough having Singer buzzing about in my mind.

Creeping through the dark bushes was no fun. I would have been lost, but Singer followed the mind she had sensed. When we reached the point where Saba had left us earlier, we turned off the path. We blundered about until we found two huts. They were screened by another fence, with a gap big enough to crawl through.

Singer went in first. I heard her gasp. Lyam, Merlinna and I crowded in behind her. I wrinkled my nose. It really did smell bad. I took the Mat-Con from my belt. *Light, little bro?* I suggested.

The MatCon transmuted some atoms into a faint beam of light.

At first, I couldn't tell what I was seeing. Then my eyes adjusted and I saw it was a clawmonster, much smaller than the one that had attacked us. I jumped back, almost falling over Lyam.

"It's dead," said Lyam.

"No," said Singer.

"It just can't move," said Merlinna harshly.

The clawmonster was crouched like a fallen statue. The MatCon light reflected in its eyes.

"What's keeping it here?" I asked.

"We para-darted it," said Noko's voice from behind us. "I told you to stay out of here."

"Why are you keeping this creature like this?" asked Singer.

"Told you we had a good way to check for poisons. If it can eat it, we can eat it," said Noko, "We're farming it too. Good idea, right? When it grows a bit it will lay eggs and we'll eat them. Or we might hatch some and farm those too."

"But it can't move!" I said.

Noko laughed. "Even little ones are nasty." He prodded the

clawmonster with his toe. "This is the safest way to deal with them." The monster twitched its tail. "Time for another dose," said Noko. He took the blowpipe out of his belt. The monster moaned.

"You don't keep it paralysed all the time, do you?" Lyam sounded as shocked as I felt.

Noko grinned at us. "You were happy for me to knock that other one out! Stand back or I might hit one of you by mistake."

We left the hut in a hurry.

In seconds Noko joined us. "I hope you're not going to be silly," he said. "It's only a monster. It would kill you if it got the chance."

"I suppose so," I said.

(After all, Noko still had the para-dart blowpipe in his hand.)

"Come back to the stockade," he said.

"We'll go to our ship," I said. Noko shrugged. "Go ahead, if you like... That monster you met before will be very pleased to see you."

We went back to the stockade.

I didn't sleep well. Every time I closed my eyes I heard the computer voice I'd heard before. *Bad, bad.* I didn't know where it was coming from but it made me uneasy.

"We've got to get away from here," muttered Lyam.

"Yes," I said. "But how?"

Then things got worse. Singer contacted me. *Pace.*

I groaned.

There was something in the other cell.

What? I said, although I really didn't want to know.

Human, said Singer. *Afraid.*

After that, I didn't sleep at all.

I felt bug-eyed with tiredness by the time the sun came up, but all the Stockaders were perfectly cheerful. They didn't seem to mind that we'd seen the monster.

"You'd better stay away from there in future, unless one of us is with you," said Noko.

"Why? Do you have other monsters in there?" asked Lyam.

Noko laughed and winked at Saba.

"Sure," said Saba. "There's more than one kind of monster." He looked at Noko. "Should we show them?"

Noko seemed to consider. "Why not?"

In daylight, the path looked less spooky but I had a horrible sinking feeling in my stomach. Seeing a monster paralysed in a cell was bad enough, but humans? Besides that, I had a nasty feeling I knew which human we were going to see.

Noko grinned as he stood back to let us crawl into the second cell. "Say hello to our new Stockaders!" he said, but he wasn't talking to us.

The person he was talking to couldn't answer him. She was paralysed, like the clawmonster.

I swallowed hard. Not only was she human, as Singer had said, but we knew her. This was Farla Fettleman of EarthNet.

chapter 6

ArkMa Takes a Hand

If I was shocked to see Farla, I was even more shocked when Singer laughed.

"Look who it is!" she chuckled, pointing.

Farla stared at us and moaned.

Noko held up his blowpipe where she could see it. She closed her eyes.

"Farla Fettleman!" said Singer, still laughing. She turned to Noko and Saba. "I see what you mean by more than one kind of monster." She spun back to the EarthNet agent. "So, how does it feel, Farla? You're always trying to grab us. Now someone has grabbed you!"

Of course, the rest of us joined in with what Singer was doing. Arkies always act as a team.

I laughed. "How long are you going to keep her here?"

Saba shrugged. "She's our insurance against anyone else interfering."

"Well, don't feed her monster eggs," I said. "She's nasty enough already."

I turned and ducked back out of the cell, into the fresh air. The others followed.

"So, have you thought any more about joining us?" asked Noko.

I glanced around at the others. "I don't know. What do you think, Singer?"

"I suppose we should," said Singer. "After all, Arkies' mission is to find S-R planets ... so you might say we've done our job. And you've sorted out the EarthNet problem."

Lyam and Merlinna nodded.

"Good!" said Noko. "Let's get you settled in, then. First step – get your gear from your ship."

"But how can we get up there?" I asked. "And what about the monster?"

"The one that attacked you?" Noko laughed. "What do you think was in your supper bowls?"

The Stockaders went to work, using their MatCon to convert a tree into a kind of ladder.

"I'll have to go first," I said. "ArkMa doesn't like strangers in the ship."

"Ark who?" said Webe.

"ArkMa," said Singer. "That's what our silly old shipbrain likes to be called. Didn't yours have a name?"

"We left it on silent mode most of the time," said Webe. "It kept saying we were … how'd it go, Noko?"

Noko took a deep breath. "Bad! Bad!" he said in a squeaky voice.

"That's it!" said Webe and laughed. "Bad! Bad! So of course, we switched it off."

So! It was the Stockaders' Ark I'd been hearing in the night! She was switched off but I must have been close enough to her to pick up some of her thoughts.

"Go on," said Noko. "Switch your shipbrain off quickly and get your gear. Make sure you don't give it a chance to send off any alarm."

I had to think really fast. For once I was

glad I was clumsy. That gave me an excuse to climb slowly.

ArkMa? I thought. *Talk to me quietly.*

Pace, where have you been? I told you—

We're in trouble, ArkMa. There are four Arkies here who have gone bad. They think we're joining them. They've switched their shipbrain off. Can you contact her?

"Hurry up!" yelled Noko as I put my foot on the last rung.

"I'm trying – AGHHH!" I let myself slip down a bit.

"Pace, you're so stupid," yelled Merlinna. I heard her telling Noko and the others a long story about how I'd messed up a landing and nearly tipped *Ark3* over a cliff.

Yes, said ArkMa. *But what then?*

I sighed. I had hoped ArkMa would solve our problems.

Can you link to her mind the same way you link to a docking beacon? I asked as I scrambled into the hatch. *She's switched off, but can you do anything?*

ArkMa was silent for a second ... and then I almost fell out of the hatch as a scream of ship-talk hit my mind.

The Stockaders' Ark was furious with them. She told ArkMa all about it in a great blast of information that nearly blew my ears off. She only calmed down when ArkMa told her I was part of their link.

Apologies, Arkie Pace, said the Ark. Then she added: *What can we do?*

You could take them off the planet, I suggested. I thought that was the best thing.

"Hurry up, Pace!" yelled Merlinna.

"I'm coming!" I scooped up an armful of things I figured we could spare and threw them out of the hatch.

They won't hear me. They won't obey me. Bad! Bad!

The poor Ark brain was almost screaming again.

I can help you, dear, said ArkMa. *If we stay linked, I can override the switches. They cannot switch me off.*

But what then? I could see how it would work. ArkMa could act as brain for the other ship and take the Stockaders back to Earth. But for either ArkMa or the other ship to do anything the Stockaders would have to be inside their own Ark.

Pace? ArkMa was nagging me. *You will have to get them inside. It's up to you.*

Great, I thought. *Just great!*

While I tossed gear out of *Ark3* I went over all kinds of ideas. Could I set Farla Fettleman free and then have her take the Stockaders back to Earth?

I liked that idea but the Stockaders had beaten Farla once. And, if Farla was loose, she'd grab me and the others as well as – or instead of – the Stockaders. As far as EarthNet was concerned, no Arkie was a good Arkie.

"Hurry!" yelled Merlinna again.

Pace? What's going on? asked Singer.

We must get them into their Ark, I said. *Let the others know.*

chapter 7

The Trap

"**W**hew! I nearly forgot to disable the beacon trip-switch," I said as I reached the ground. I started picking up some of the gear.

"What's a beacon trip-switch?" asked Rudu.

"It's the switch that sets off a beacon if an Ark stays empty for too long," I said. "You know – the one under that panel near the viewscreen? You must have disabled yours when you got here."

I could see the Stockaders didn't know what I meant. I wasn't surprised. I'd made it up.

"Of course," said Webe.

Noko shrugged.

I knew I couldn't push the idea or the Stockaders would smell trouble.

"Is it OK to cut some vines?" I asked. "We need better sleeping places."

"Start there," said Webe, pointing to the big vine-smothered building.

"Sure," I said. I added, privately, to the MatCon, *Hey, little bro – is the Ark brain lady inside there?*

I felt the MatCon sniffing around and, then, a little click as it connected.

Bad. Bad.

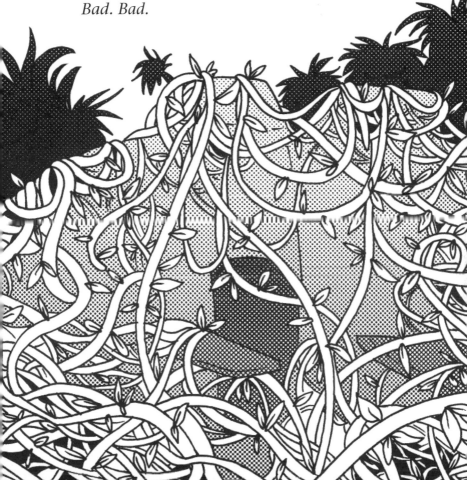

I hear you, Ma'am, I said. I snipped about and the shape of an Ark began to show through the vines. I noticed Rudu watching and grinned at him. "This is your old Ark, right? Just as well you tripped the switch or she'd have a beacon screaming soon."

Rudu came closer. "This switch," he said. "Near the viewscreen, you said?"

"That's where it is in our Ark," I said. "Was yours somewhere different?"

Rudu shrugged. "Can't remember," he said. "Have to check with Webe."

I gathered my armful of vines and took them away. *Ready, little bro?* I said to the MatCon.

I felt the MatCon making contact with ArkMa and the other Ark Lady.

Ready, Pace, said ArkMa.

I kept on with what I was doing. Out of the corner of my eye, I saw Rudu and Webe heading for their old Ark. Rudu opened the hatch and they climbed inside.

Now! I told MatCon, and I felt it set up the relay.

Yours, ArkMa! said the other ship ... and ArkMa took control and closed the hatch.

There was silence. I was sure Rudu and Webe were banging about inside, trying to use the manual switches.

Pace? Singer was touching my hand.

ArkMa has control, I said.

What about Noko and Saba?

I hope they'll get curious and climb in too...

After a while, Noko came over to me. "Pace, did you see where the others went?"

I shrugged.

"Into that big hut, I think," said Merlinna.

Noko laughed. "Hey, Saba ... I'm going into the big hut. You stay out here, OK?"

Saba nodded.

Now! I told ArkMa as Noko put his hand on the door of the hatch. I just hoped he would go in before the others gave the alarm. I thought I heard a yell but the hatch closed again behind the Stockader.

I took a deep breath and tried to look mean. I raised the MatCon. "Saba, pick up as much of this vine as you can. You're going to need it on your way to Earth."

Saba stared at me in shock.

"Now, Saba," I said. "Unless you want me to turn you into mince."

Saba turned pale. I think he really thought I would do it. I jerked the MatCon. "Now. Help him, Arkies, but don't let him grab you."

The others scooped up the cut vines and carried them over to the Ark. I got ArkMa to open the hatch just a crack.

"Noko?" I said, standing well out of range.

"What's going on?" yelled Noko.

"Listen. Get in your bunks. Roll over. Face the wall. If you don't, that hatch will seal right now and you will starve. If you do as I say, you will have food."

I heard Noko laugh. "You can't be serious, kid?"

"I am," I said. "Do it now."

I guess Noko did as I said because ArkMa cracked the door open just enough for Saba and the vines to go inside.

A minute later, the Ark lifted clear of Monster Planet and shot upwards, trailing vines. We never saw her after that but ArkMa says she got safely to Earth. I don't know what happened to the Stockaders, but I'm sure they'll never be allowed into space again.

✪ ✪ ✪

That was almost the end of our adventure. We went to see Farla before we left. The para-dart was wearing off so I was in a hurry to get clear. "If

you tell us your ship code, we can relay a call for Tench to come and collect you," I said.

Farla glared at me. "Pace, you know it is your duty to all come home with me now to be re-educated. Surely you must see—"

"Farla," I snapped, "give me the code now or you can stay here for ever with the monsters. I don't care."

Farla gave me the code.

We left Monster Planet that same day. I thought ArkMa would be mad at me about the whole adventure but she didn't say much. I guess she was too busy running two Arks that were going in different directions.

"We should never have gone there," I said aloud.

The other Arkies stared at me.

"But of course we should, Pace," said Singer. "If we hadn't, the Stockaders would still have Farla and would still be torturing monsters."

I nodded, slowly. I think Singer had a point, don't you?

MONSTER PLANET
Official Arkie report.
NOT S-R.

Monster Planet Cosmopedia

Arkie Academy Where the Arkies learned their special skills.

Arkies Teenagers with special training who act as pathfinders, seeking new Settlement-Ready planets.

Ark3 The space craft in which the Arkies travel.

ArkMa The sentient computer that flies *Ark3*. A shipbrain.

Ark Masters The heads of the Arkie programme.

Chaining Singer uses chaining (mindtalking through linked hands) in an emergency.

Didgies Indigenous inhabitants of a planet.

Docking beacon A beacon to which a shipbrain like ArkMa can lock.

EarthNet An organisation that wants the Arkies to go home.

Hatch code The typed-in code that tells ArkMa to release the hatch.

Monster Planet Cosmopedia

MatCon Matter converters, used to convert matter into useful objects – including food. Can only work if the raw materials are present.

Ship-boots Footwear worn by Arkies and EarthNet Agents.

Shipbrain The electronic mind of an Arkie ship.

Ship-suit One-piece garment used by spacers.

S-R (Settlement-Ready) Planets that have oxygen, free water, vegetation, metal and no intelligent didgies.

Tangle-line Merlinna's weapon of choice. A flicked line that entangles legs or arms and stings but does not injure.

Viewscreen Viewing hatch aboard the *Ark3*.